"Nothing but dry dirt and clear skies. Freedom so close, yet so far. Taken away by bars and chains!" Justice says sadly. A twenty two year old, light skinned male with braids, who stands five feet ten inches tall. Sentenced to three years in San Quentin for breaking and entering and a kidnapping charge. He stares out the window feeling hopeless, thinking about his fiance, Denise. A twenty one year old, caramel toned, independent black woman, with the resemblance of Kerry Washington and their three year old son Lyfe. "Don't trip...Atleast we ain't doin a letter!" His brother Kaseem replied with a smile. Kaseem, who is also doing time for the same charge, is a year older than Justice and a little bulkier. He sits there at six feet two inches, mean mugging other inmates, trying to adjust his tight handcuffs. "Aye officer....Come loosen these thangs up man!" He thinks about his pregnant girlfriend Sasha. She looks like she can be the exact twin of Lala Anthony, with twin girls growing inside her stomach. "I knew we shouldn't have did that bullshit man!" Justice whispers. "I jus got my bachelor's in physics!" "Man... You act like I ain't get mines either!" Kaseem says, cutting him off. "We still from the hood bro and these degrees ain't get none of us paid!" Kaseem leans forward. Justice shakes his head, still thinking about his fiance and son. "We made fifty racks a piece from this lick. We only doin a couple of years. Our ladies are strong man, we good!" Kaseem reassures him. The bus stops short and the driver opens the door. "How many?" The sheriff asks while the inmates look around to see the building for the first time. "Twelve men, four women!" The driver replies. The sheriff marks it down on his pad, waves the bus to move forward and the gates open. "Welcome to your new home ladies and gentlemen. Enjoy the duration of your time!" The driver says over the speaker as he drives around to the side of the building to drop off the women first. "Show me a titty?" One of the inmates shouted. The women looked scared straight. None of them responded. The bus went back in motion and Justice started looking at all of the mens faces, "Scary, huh?" Kaseem asked while trying to look tough. This was their first time ever being in jail and now, they would have to live there for the next three years. "Na...Not really. As long as noone messes with us, I'm good!" Justice replies as he daps up Kaseem. They exit the bus and instantly smell rust from old bars and fresh pepper spray. "To the right!" A correction officer yells to the inmates while they walk into the building and are handed a change of clothes and a towel. The officer reads them the rules and they all get naked and walk into the shower. They hop out a few minutes later, get dressed and head to their new rooms. "I swear these officers are gay!" Kaseem said angrily. "Why is that?" Justice asks. "Everyday they make men lift their sac and spread their cheeks!" Justice shakes his head and laughs. "You think this gon be our room for the time being?" "I don't know!" Kaseem replies as he places his cup and spoon, he just stole, on the desk and hops on the top bunk. Justice watches as the door closes. "We're officially locked down!" "Yea..... Tomorrow, I'ma hop on the phone and call Sasha!" Kaseem replies cutting him off. Justice lays on his bunk and thinks about his family as he falls asleep......

......"TAP TAP TAP!" The officer bangs his keys against the bars of the door, Echoeing through the halls. Justice and Kaseem quickly wake up, "What the hell!" Kaseem shouts. "Wake up inmates, you're being transferred!" Justice wipes his eyes, "What time is it?" "Time for you to get your shit and get out!" The officer replied. Kaseem hops down off the bunk, slowly grabs his stuff and waits for Justice. " Don't worry about your girl friend, he'll be fine...Now move before I bring you to the hole!" The officer shouts. Kaseem walks up to the officer and says, "You betta watch ya mouth, dat's my brother!" "Oh...So, you keep it in the family, huh? Move!" The officer replies. Justice grabs his stuff and walks behind Kaseem. They head down the hallway and pass a clock on the wall.

"2:15am...Damn!" Justice whispers. They walk past a name plate on the corner wall that says, WEST WING. Justice looks down there and sees a glass wall with inmates in their rooms yelling, "Fresh Meat!" "Keep movin!" The officer says. They turn right down the hall and see an inmate sweeping and another mopping. Kaseem hears the broom drop and the dark skinned brother yells, "Fruit Town Blood!" Justice looks at Kaseem nervously and asks, "You know him?" Kaseem smiles and simply replies, "Hell naw... He jus tryna scare us!" They walk past another name plate that says, EAST WING. They both looked down the hallway and seen nothing but darkness and quietness. "Here you go!" The officer said, pointing to THE SYSTEM plate. Justice was relieved that they weren't going into the EAST WING. "You're room 102!" The officer gave Justice a slip of paper and said, "Right bunk!" Justice took the slip and walked along the left wall until the block went dark. He took a left and seen light again. "207, upstairs!" Kaseem snatched the slip and didn't hesitate to hit the stairs. " Right bunk Kaseem!" The officer yelled. "Fuck you!" He replied as he disappeared into the darkness......

......As Justice gets closer to his room, he hears noises. "Oh yes, uh huh, deeper... Deeper!" "What the hell!" Justice whispers as he starts to get nervous. " Oh my god, yes!" Justice turns into his room and sees a big black muscle head Ving Rhames looking inmate blowing the back out of a female correctional officer. " The hell you starin at?" The inmate asks as he keeps pumping into the officer. Justice turns around and sits outside of the cell, relieved that it wasn't two guys going at it. "I'm bouta cum, oh my god... I'm cumming!" The officer shouts as she squirts all over him and down her legs. The inmate grabs her hair and says, "Me too!" He lifts his leg and puts it on the toilet and starts long stroking. Eight pumps later, he busts all inside her. He slaps her butt, then quickly puts his clothes on. Justice stands up and walks back into the cell and places his stuff on his bunk. "Aye, lil nigga. I find out you a rat, what you saw is gon happen to you!" The officer fixed her pants and her hair and simply replied, "Don't worry baby, I'ma get his paperwork!" She slowly jiggled her onion booty out the room and disappeared. "It's none of my business!" Justice says as he lays down on his bunk and tries to sleep with one eye open. "The name is Travis, but you can call me Mr. leave me the fuck alone!" Justrice smiled and replied, "I can dig it!" He turned over and went to sleep......

......"The hell I look like!" Kaseem whispered angrily as he reached across the wall, looking for the light switch. "Don't turn on the light!" A voice quickly shouted. Kaseem dropped his stuff, turned the light on and seen a young black kid sitting on the toilet. "Why you turn on the light for? Damn!" The kid said pissed off. " Shut up before I choke you out on that seat!" Kaseem replied as he picked up his stuff and placed it on his bunk. He turned around and seen plenty of graffiti and drawings around the room. "You did all of this?" The kid looked at Kaseem and simply replied, "Do you mind?" Kaseem shook his head, walked towards the door, then quickly turned around and put the kid in a sleeper hold. "Listen...I don't care what you're here for, but that attitude is gonna stop, you hear me?" Kaseem whispered as he tightened his grip. The kid, tapping rapidly on Kaseem's arm, was losing his breath very fast. Kaseem stood the kid up and tightened all the way, until he seen the kids arm drop. Kaseem let the kid drop to the floor with his pants down. "What's that smell?" He asked himself while looking around. He noticed a stain on his pants. "Oh hell naw!" The kid took a dump on Kaseem while falling asleep. "You gon clean all dis up when you wake up!" He said while changing his clothes. Kaseem sat on his bunk, seen the kids snacks, grabbed them and turned on the kids television. About an hour later, the kid woke up. "What did you do to me?" The kid shouted, confused. "Calm down!" Kaseem replied while eating the kids doritos. The kid checks himself to see if he's been violated. "Don't worry. You ain't been penetrated!" Kaseem says smiling. "You were jus tryna act tough so, I put you to sleep!" The kid started getting nervous. "What's your name ?" Kaseem asks as he starts to sit up. "Davon!" "Well, Davon...Here's the deal. Your store order every week, mine. I control the tv. All your cosmetics, mine!" "What?" Davon asked while sitting up. "You must be out your!" Kaseem cut Davon off with a quick jab to his chin. Davon's face hit the toilet and blood started dripping from his lip. "Oh kayyy. Damn!" Davon replied holding his face. "How old are you?" Kaseem asked while grabbing Davon's chili fritos. "Nineteen!" Kaseem gets up and grabs Davon's bed, puts it under his bed and wraps his sheet around it. He throws Davon his pillow and blanket and tells him to sleep on the floor after he cleans everything up. Ten minutes later, Davon lays the blanket down on the floor and fluffs his pillow. "What are you here for?" Kaseem asks. "Not registering!" Kaseem scratches his head and replies, "Not registering what? A car? Your license? I don't understand!" Davon pushes himself all the way back to the door and starts shaking. "Uh...Uh... Sex offender!" He replies in a very low tone. Well, not low enough because Kaseem heard it very clear. He jumped up. Davon covered his face and curled up like a fetus. Kaseem grabbed Davon's pillow and blanket and placed it on his bed. He quickly went over to Davon and stood there until he slowly moved his hands. "How old was she?"

Kaseem asked in an evil tone. Davon, scared straight, whispered, "Twelve... But she looked twenty one!" And was quickly interupted with a field goal kick to his chin. Instantly knocking him out. Snoring to the max, Kaseem leaned over him and whispered, "I'ma make your life a living hell!"......

4 MONTHS LATER

JUSTICE AND KASEEM

......"Yo Jus, wake up man... It's breakfast time. Gimme ya cereal!" Kaseem said as he wipes his face. Justice yawns and replies, "Gotta get ya weight up, huh?" Kaseem makes a stank face. "Na. You gotta get your toothpaste up and calm dat breath down!" They both laugh as Kaseem exits the room. A couple minutes later, Justice is ready and heads out. He rushes down the hall and sees people entering the chow hall. "What up tho!" Kaseem yells with his hands up, waiting for Justice to cut in front of twenty people. Justice makes his way down the line and bumps into someone, but keeps it moving. "Fuck's yo matter?" The man says. Justice pays no mind to it. He grabs his tray and walks to find Kaseem at a full table. "Damn!" He whispers. Justice looks and sees a table two rows away from Kaseem, so he goes there and quickly cracks open his milk. "Yup, lemme get dat and dat, two milks, yup!" Kaseem says smiling while food is being passed over to his tray. He packs his cereal down, pours two cartons of milk into it and starts to grub. All of a sudden, someone yells, "Fruit town blood!" Kaseem gets a swift punch to the left side of his face, knocking the spoon, food and milk out of his mouth. Justice slowly looks to see what the commotion is about and he notices Kaseem blocking blows to his head, while regaining his balance. "Oh shit!" Justice quickly jumps up, climbs on the table and hops, from table to table, to his brother. Justice lands a hard left kick to the back of the man's head and falls on him. "Bitch ass nigga!" Justice yells as he gets up and starts beating on the guy. Kaseem gets up and swiftly kicks the man in his face, knocking out a tooth with squirts of blood. They both continue kicking the man, until a squad of correctional officers come breaking them up by spraying them with pepper spray. They quickly lay them on the floor, cuff them and bring all three to the hole. About ten minutes later, after hosing them down and giving them segregation clothes, they're sent to the captains office, one by one. The man that got jumped went first. "So... Dante Patrick!" The captain said shaking his head in disbelief. "Where do I start? I know you started this. This is your fourth fight in six months. Do I need to put you in the dungeon?" "I don't give a fuck!" Dante replied. "Cuz, when I get out, I'ma get at them again. They here for kidnapping my cousin!" "Everyone's your cousin Patrick!" Captain replied cutting him off. "What's it gonna take for you to stop fighting and causing riots?" "Put Kaseem in WEST WING with me and my crew?" Dante quickly replies. "Absolutely not!" The captain banged on the desk. "Your crew will kill him. What about his brother retaliating?" "Aiight!" Dante said calmly. " Here's the deal... You bring him in with us and we won't kill him. Jus make his life a living hell. If not, we'll jus tie your wife up again. This time,we'll have your daughter watch her get tortured!" The captain rubs his beard nervously. "Fine...Hurry up and get outta my office!" A few minutes later, Kaseem walks in looking like he just won the UFC championship belt. "Sit down Mr. Cosgrove!" The captain said staring at his file on the computer. Kaseem leans up against the wall and simply replies, "Do wut you gotta do, I'm still doin time!" The captain looked at Kaseem, knowing he wasn't going to get anything else out of him, simply says, "You leave me no choice!" The captain waves Kaseem out of the office and Justice walks right in. He immediately goes to sit in the chair, but leans it back on two legs. "Justice Cosgrove!" The captain says. "This is your first time in jail I presume!" Justice sits up and smoothly replies, "It doesn't mean I'm scared. It jus means don't mess with me and I won't mess with you!" The captain smiles and replies, "It's funny because on camera, noone was messing with you when your brother was getting beat down!" Justice stares at him for a moment, then smirks. "You guys aren't in any gangs but, you pissed off a blood gang member. Retaliation is coming. What do you plan on doing about it?" The captain asked while folding his hands together. "Like I said!" Justice gets up and heads toward the door, "You don't mess with me and I won't mess with you!" Justice opens the door and the captain shouts, "We're not done!" Justice looks at the captain, "I'm in trouble for this, right?" "Yes!" The captain replies. "Then we're done!" Justice says as he closes the door and gets cuffed. The next morning, all three get released but, Justice is sent to EAST WING. Kaseem and Dante are sent to WEST WING and are mean mugging each other the whole time.

"Welcome to my house baby gurl!" Dante says as he's being uncuffed. As soon as Kaseem gets his left wrist out, he back hands Dante like a dirty whore. The correctional officer uncuffs Kaseem's right hand and walks away slowly, closes the door behind him and laughs. Kaseem suddenly looks confused. "Ooh. You shouldn't have!" Dante replies smiling, wiping the blood off his busted lip. Kaseem spots three men getting up and coming toward him so, he backs up towards the door. "Nowhere to hide baby gurl!" Dante says laughing. Kaseem throws his fists up, looking around but, doesn't see Justice. He focuses on Dante and whispers, "This is gonna be a long two and a half years!"......

......Justice gets to his room but, is quickly stopped by three men. "Are you a ripper?" One of the men asked. "What's that?" He replied confused. "Are you a rat?" The same man asked. Justice started getting angry. "Hell no!" A big light skinned man came walking out from behind them, kinda looking like Dwayne "The Rock" Johnson. He spoke in a calm voice. "It's ok. I know him!" The big guy pushes through the men and grabs Justice on his shoulder firmly. "Don't be afraid, noone's gonna hurt you. Put your stuff over here to the left and just relax!" Justice, looking a little nervous, just replies, "Aiight!" He puts his stuff down and sits on his bunk. "The name is Nate. The crew calls me O.G Loc from C-side!" Justice looks at him and realizes that there's blue everywhere. Before he spoke, Nate already cut him off. "I know everything about you and your wild brother Kaseem. I know about your fiance' Denise and his girlfriend Sasha, with the twins they're about to have soon!" Justice, looking shocked and amazed, was wondering how he knew so much. *"I know everything about your case, even the people you've kidnapped!" "Ear to the streets, huh?" Justice asked with a smirk. "Let's jus say, when people sleep, I know what they're dreaming about!" Nate replied giving Justice a honey bun. Justice, now paranoid, was trying to think of a way to get out of the room. "Why did they split us up?" He asked Nate, accepting the honey bun and slowly eating it. Nate looks at Justice and leans forward, "The captain, not the warden, runs this place. The piru's have a tight grip on him. Me, on the other hand, I keep the peace, you know. A little give and take!" "So, you split us up?" Justice asked stuffing his face. "I thought you were smarter than that! You forgot about your fight with the blood in the cafeteria. That's their payment and they don't want you to retaliate!" Justice starts to get angry. "That's my brother! He yells. "I'm not jus* gonna sit here while they get away with this!" He starts pacing back and forth. "Calm down, you have a visit in a couple of hours. Go take a shower and get ready. Just relax, when you come back, I'll help you get your revenge!......

JUSTICE AND DENISE

......Justice stands at the gate while waiting for the aofficer to uncuff him. Moments later, the gate opens up and he walks eight stalls down to the left and sees his fiance' Denise and his son Lyfe waving at him through the four inch thick bulletproof glass window. Justice sits down and quickly grabs the phone and smiles as tears start to fall. "Hey beautiful!" "Hey honey, how you holding up in there?" Denise replies as tears of joy runs down her face but, is quickly interupted by their son Lyfe. Lyfe climbs up and down on the table, banging on the glass, waving. "Hi daddy!" "You're all he talks about. Everything he does, everything he learns, he can't wait to show and tell you!" Justice puts his hand on the glass and Lyfe slaps it and tries to squeeze it. "I miss you guys so much!" Justice said sadly. "Two years and we'll be outta hea!" Denise quickly cuts him off, "Why are you in grey? Last time you were in blue!" Justice simply replies, "Kaseem got into it with someone and the next thing you know, we get seperated!" "So, you can't see him anymore?" She asked concerned. "Only at chow but, after sixty days, I can transfer to his wing!"

Lyfe keeps banging on the glass. "Hold on baby, I'ma give the phone to Lyfe!" "Hi daddy!" Lyfe says properly as he sits correctly and starts behaving. "Hey big man. You being good and listening to mommy?" "Daddy!" Lyfe quickly cuts him off. "You told me to be the man of the house, right dad? So, mommy listens to me. I tell mommy to have a good day at work and she does. When she asks me what I learned in school, I tell her!" "So, what did you learn in school then, Mr. man of the house?" Justice asked smiling. Denise smiled and pointed at Lyfe while shaking her head up and down. "I learned that there are twenty six letters in the alphabet. Spanish people, for some reason, don't know their b's from their v's and Jamaican people only use thirteen letters out of twenty six so, they only say half of each word daddy. I don't understand!" He shrugs his little shoulders. Denise and Justice laugh histerically. "You're very smart son, don't grow up too fast!" " I won't dad!" Lyfe replied. "I'ma stay three years old until you get out so, we can continue our fun from where we left off!" A tear fell hard from Justice's face onto the table before he even had a chance to realize it. "Five minutes!" The officer yells to Justice, cutting his normal visiting time from twenty five to ten. "What's that all about?" Denise asked as she quickly snatched the phone from Lyfe. "We're in gang units so, we get shorter time!" He replies looking over his shoulder. "Listen baby. I love you and miss you so much. The letters and pictures keep my mind away from *this place. I wait everyday for mail to slide under my door. I can't wait to be a family with you two again!" "Don't worry honey, I'll keep'em coming!" Denise replied smiling while a few tears dropped. "Me too daddy. I can tie my shoes see!" He puts the phone down and starts to tie them. Denise grabs the phone again. "He's too damn smart!" "Yes he is!" Justice replies. "Baby...I love you so much. Hurry up and come home to us , ok! We love you and we'll see you next week!" Denise blew kisses and Lyfe kept trying to tie his shoe. The officer came and grabbed Justice by the arm and rushed him back for emergency lock down. Heading back, he didn't want to let go of those moments of freedom he had with his family. Forced to lock that memory in his emotional* vault, Justice had to walk back into the jungle......

KASEEM

......Dante sends a quick left jab straight to Kaseem's nose. Blood starts leaking but, he's unfazed. Kaseem grabs Dante's throat and pushes him back, swings on the guy to the left of him and catches him on the side of his forehead. "Ya'll ain't tough!" Kaseem says laughing. The guy, on the other side, tries to grab Kaseem. He lets go of Dante and two pieces the guy in the gut, followed by an uppercut. Dante secretly pulls out a shank and pokes Kaseem in the right side of his stomach. "Ahh... Son of a!"

Kaseem yells, grabbing Dante with the shank still inside of him, head butts him then throws him to the ground. The two guys jump on Kaseem and tries to hold him down. "Got you now fresh meat!" One guy whispers in his ear. The other guy shoves the shank further inside. "Ahhhh!" Kaseem yells. Dante gets up and walks over to Kaseem, while wiping his face, "You in my house now, baby girl!" Dante goes to kick him but, Kaseem grabs his foot. "Get him!" Dante yells nervously. With his second wind, Kaseem pushes the two guys off him, while still holding Dante, head butts him again and quickly pulls out the shank. The two guys tackle Kaseem again but, they ended up at a table. "Get off me you faggot ass nigga!" Kaseem yells as he looks around and sees about thirty other inmates standing around amazed. One guy punches Kaseem in the back of the head, trying to knock him out but, it doesn't work. He takes the shank and swings back. "Ahh.. My shoulder!" The guy crys out. Searching for Dante, Kaseem is still fighting off the other guy. Kaseem takes a deep breath and stands up, with the guy on his back, flips him over onto the table. "BOOM!" The whole block echoed and you can hear everyone screaming, "Oh shit! Damn! Dis niggas a beast!" Kaseem holds the side of his stomach, trying to stop the bleeding. The guy with the shank in his shoulder is sitting on the floor, trying to take the shank out and Dante is nowhere to be found. Kaseem drags the guy off the table, onto the floor and field goal kicks him in the sid eof his face. Dante finally creeps out of the crowd with a long knife. "This is it for you!" Kaseem just laughs and replies, "Scary ass...I'ma take dat from you and put you over my knee!" Dante starts swinging like crazy as Kaseem backs up towards the glass wall. "This isn't a fair fight!" Dante says smiling as he starts to back up into a corner. " "Here!" Dante throws down the knife and says, "Now it's fair!" Kaseem, unaware of the inmates mumbling in the background, feels something isn't right. A man, standing 6'6, looking like the incredible hulk, with big letters CB tatted across his face, sneeks up on him and quickly puts Kaseem in a sleeper hold. Dante smiled, rubbing his hands together. "Don't worry, get you some rest. We'll take care of your lady and *your twins!" Kaseem couldn't fight much longer. He started seeing white spots then, he felt his legs starting to give out. "Fa fa fa, ga ga ga!" Only spit and half words Kaseem could release before he was completely out cold. "Stop being a girl...Hurry up and take that shank out and help me with Kaseem's body!" Dante said, getting ready to grab his feet. "O.G. Master Kody....Want us to put him near the door?" The incredible hulk looking guy smiles the replies in a deep voice, "Naw...Ya'll three put him in my room and wait there until he wakes up!"......*

SASHA

......"We gon need to get a bigger place once you girls come out!" Sasha says, trying to sit down sideways in the living room. "DING DONG!" "Aww man...What is it now!" Trying to get up, the doorbell rings continously. "I'm comin, I'm comin!" She shouts. She makes it to the door and opens it. "Hello! I'm Jessica. I'm ten and this is Maria. She's eleven and we're selling girl scout cookies!" Sasha rubs her stomach to calm the twins down and asks, "What kind of cookies are you selling?" The girls, dressed in their green outfits, drag their green wagon, with all different types of cookies, up to the door. "Yum!" Sasha replies. "Come on in girls, lemme grab my wallet, I'll be right back!" Sasha waddles away slowly. The girls step into the house but, leaves the door halfway open. Sasha returns a couple minutes later with her purse and a hundred dollar bill in her hand.

"Now, do you have any Junior Mints?" The girls quickly respond, "Yes!" With a smile, they quickly pull out their .22 caliber pistols from their skirts. "You kids need to stop. You can't be this serious!" Sasha replies upset, thinking it's a simple robbery. "No. This is for Kaseem!" Jessica says as she swiftly kicks Sasha in the bottom of her stomach with her right boot. "Oh damn!" Sasha yells, leaning forward and grabbing her stomach with both hands. Maria hits Sasha in the face with her gun then, searches through the wagon for handcuffs. "Who sent you?" Sasha demanded, spitting up blood. "Kody!" A deep voice replied as a man stepped into the house and closed the door. Sasha, still holding her stomach, tries to make it to her couch but, gets stopped by the girls. "Now...I'ma cuff your hands behind your back. If you put up a fight, it would only get worse!" Jessica said smiling.

Sasha didn't know what was going on. Just the thought of them knowing Kaseem, Sasha knew it wasn't going to end well for her. She complied with the cuffs behind her back and Jessica softly asks,"It isn't too tight, is it?" Sasha simply replied, "No!" Jessica shook her head at Maria. Maria walks in front of Sasha and says, "Here...Let me help you sit down!" Then quickly field goal kicks her in the side of her stomach. Sasha screams out and drops to her knees. The man walks over to Sasha, kneels down and starts to whisper, "Don't worry, when we're done with you, you can have Kaseem to thank!" Sasha, trying hard to breathe, drools on herself as tears fall down her face. She sees blood leaking from her pants. "I hope whatever he did to you was worth it!" The man looks at Sasha then tells the girls to get in the car. They leave, closing the door behind them. He locks the door and says, "Now, what I'm gonna need you to do is take a deep breath cus this is gonna hurt. Badly!" He goes to get a broom then walks over to her. Sasha leans against the couch, trying to regain strength. He grabs her pants, pulls them down then rips them off. Blood starts dripping onto her carpet. "You don't want your kids to see how sick and twisted you are?" Sasha asked painfully. "No...They're not my kids. I jus found them, gave them 200 hundred each and told them to do what I say!" The man replied as he pulled down her panties and grabbed the broom. He stood up, put his foot on her neck and shoved her head down into the corner of the couch and the floor. "Any last words?" He asked as he pulled a small torch from his left pants pocket and lit the end of the broom on fire. "Go to hell!" She mumbled. He blew the lit end of the broom off, aimed it at her anal cavity, took *his foot off her neck and shoved the broom as far in as he could until Sasha stopped screaming......*

JUSTICE

......After being rushed out of the visit for emergency lock down, Justice was confused onto what was happening. He seen a dozen officers in riot gear rushing towards him. "Get Back!" The officer that was bringing him to his cell said as he pushed Justice up against the wall. "What's happening?" The officer didn't respond. He just watched as the last officer past them and disappeared around the corner. "Let's go!" The officer said as he quickly pulled out his night stick and hits Justice in the stomach so hard he falls to his knees. Justice, now drooling and bent over, tried to gasp for air. A long shiny

boot appeared out of nowhere and hit Justice clean in his left cheek. Justice fell to the side and leaned against the wall helpless. "What the!" Justice says trying to gasp for more air as blood starts spilling from his mouth. He seen the night stick aim at his face. Justice tried to block it then, he heard a crack. "Ahhh!" Justice screams. "You broke my wrist!" The officer smiles and replies, "This is what happens when you assault an officer!" The officer then pulls Justice away from the wall, kicks him in the stomach again and starts wailing on his back with the night stick. Justice thought he was going to die. He kept trying to get up but, every hit felt like a pound of cement blocks. He gave up and laid there, accepting death, until he seen a young man in the distance. "Justice...Justice, wake up!" The young man said as he grabbed the keys off the officer and started to uncuff him. The officer instantly fell to the floor and blood *started running from his neck. "Come on. I got you!" The young man said to Justice while picking him up. Justice, trying to regain his strength, asks, "What?" In a low tone. "Don't trip. I'ma get you healed and everything's gonna be cophistetic!" The young man replied. "I'm Monty by the way!" He brought Justice all the way to the hospital, sat there and waited, so noone would mess with him......*

KASEEM

......"Wake up, baby gurl!" Dante says laughing as he splashes water on Kaseem. O.G. Master Kody stands guard inside his room waiting patiently. The two guys are ready to grab Kaseem as soon as he wakes up. Kaseem jumps up and leans back, "What the!" Kaseem starts kicking at all

three of them. "Hold him down!" Dante replies excitedly. Kaseem throws a fast hook at Dante, catching him in his chin. The two guys manage to hold him down. "Now, I'm not gonna be so nice!" Dante replied holding his face. He hits Kaseem with two quick jabs to his left eye. "Turn him over!" O.G. Master Kody says as he starts to hand them ripped sheets. They tie Kaseem to the bed. "Awww, hell naw!" He yells, trying to yank the sheets off him but, it's too late. "Ha ha ha!" Dante laughs as he starts tieing his legs to each corner of the bunk. "Move!" O.G. Master Kody shouts. "I'm bouta hea you sing like Alicia Keys!" He grabs his knife, cuts open Kaseem's pants and pulls them off. "Gimme the vaseline!" He says to Dante. "Homo thugs!" Kaseem shouts as he keeps trying to break free. Dante whips out his piece and slaps Kaseem in the face with it. "You piece of shit. I'ma kill you first!" Kaseem yells as he struggles to break free again. "Now...We can do this the hard way!" O.G. Master Kody says grinning. "And wut's the easy way?" Kaseem asked pissed off. O.G. Master Kody swipes the vaseline with his left hand , slides it between Kaseem's cheeks and quickly forces himself inside him. "Haaaaaa!" Kaseem yells, trying to breathe, realizing this is happening to him. O.G. Master Kody whispers in Kaseem's ear, "That was the easy way!" He continues to pump him a few times until he grabs Kaseem's head and forces him to look at Dante. "He's next!" O.G. Master Kody says devilishly. Dante smiles. The guys are still holding him down. O.G. Master Kody releases inside of him, then says, "Don't worry...You're not gonna be my bitch...But you will be Dante's!" Dante, wrapping sandpaper around his piece, grabs a towel and starts wiping Kaseem up. Kaseem is in tears. "I'ma kill each and everyone of you!" As soon as he finished with his sentence, he felt a burning sensation from his anal cavity all the way to his throat. "Yea, baby gurl...You feel me?" Dante whispers in Kaseem's ear. Kaseem screams out in pain. He passes out and the guys take turns getting oral from Kaseem until his mouth fills up. O.G. Master Kody steps out of the room. The other inmates, terrified, listening to the horror and petrified to even speak. Some go in their rooms, others continue to play dominoes and cards and act like everything is normal!......

ONE MONTH LATER

SASHA AND DENISE

......The sun shines bright through the shades onto Sasha as she lays in the hospital bed sleep. Filled with tubes, Denise and Lyfe sit in the chair facing her. "I'm hungry mommy. When aunty Sasha wakes up, can we eat?" Lyfe asks rubbing his stomach. Denise smiles and rubs his back. "Yes honey, we will!" Just then, a nurse comes in to check on Sasha. "Good afternoon!" She says smiling, checking the tubes and reading the heart rate machine. The nurse checks the bags and switches them. She pulls out a syringe and a little bottle. "What is she doing mommy?" Lyfe asks. Denise softly replies, "She's jus makin sure auntie Sasha has her fluids and gives her medicine so, she can heal faster!" Lyfe looks at the nurse and sees that the bottle has a skull with a red x behind it. "What does that do?" Lyfe asks the nurse, pointing to the bottle in her hand.

Denise, unaware of what's going on, simply tells Lyfe to leave the nurse alone and let her do her job. "But mommy, I seen on tv that skulls and bones are bad and there's people in suits and words like caution!" "Your son is very smart, huh?" The nurse replied, quickly cutting him off. She placed the bottle in her pocket, flicked the syringe and began to walk over to Sasha. "C'mon honey, sit on my lap. Let the nurse do her job!" Denise said grabbing him and putting him on her left leg. Lyfe quickly leans over and digs in her pocket. "What's wrong with you. Stop it or else you're not playing with your toys when you get home!" Upset with Lyfe, Denise puts him down and quickly grabs the bottle he was spinning in his hand. "Cyanide!" Denise shouts as she drops the bottle and pushes the nurse away from Sasha. "What the hell are you doing?" Denise yells. The nurse smiles ajkl;\nd replies, "My job!" The nurse pushes Denise and pulls out her black

.380. She points it at Lyfe as he covers his ears. He sees his mother knock the gun out of the nurses hand and sees it spinning in his direction. Denise gives the nurse a hard jab to her chin and grabs her hair. Lyfe grabs the gun and looks at it. The nurse punches Denise in her stomach, twice, then in her face. Denise yells, "I eat those for breakfast!" She grabs the nurses face and slams it hard against her knee. Instantly breaking her nose. Blood starts gushing. Lyfe points the gun at the nurse and walks up to her. He sees her bringing her arm back to hit his mom and, "POW!" Lyfe shoots the nurse in her right butt cheek. The nurse screams out. "LYFE!" Denise yells as she quickly runs to him and snatches the gun away. "Power Rangers mommy!" Lyfe says with a smile. Denise hugs him extra hard and tight. She picks him up. "You're not watching anymore Power Rangers!" Denise looks at the nurse bleeding all over the floor. She walks over to

Sasha and pulls out the needles from her arm. "I hope it's not too late!" She whispers. Two other nurses rush in to see what the noise was about. "Call the police!" Denise shouts to them as she puts Lyfe down. She looks at the bed and sees the syringe. She picks it up and it's still full. "The same people that sent you are the same people that did this to her, huh?" She asked the nurse, knowing she wasn't going to get an answer. The nurse laughs, then replies, "It's only a matter of time until you get the same treatment!"......

JUSTICE

......"It's only bruised ribs!" Nate said to Justice as he sees him looking depressed. "You need to get in the shower. You're starting to smell like Taz!" "Who's dat?"

Justice replies, looking confused. "Oh, jus a young nobody who thinks he can draw and tattoo. He walks around like he's tough but, he gave two white boys oral for some color pencils and drawing paper!" Nate said laughing. "What does that have to do with him stinking?" Nate sits up and looks at Justice with a death stare. "Cuz, ever since he got his manhood taken in the shower, he's never been the same!" "Damn...Why did that happen to him?" Justice asked curiously. Nate fell back and simply replied, "Level three sex offender. His real name is Davon!" Justice shakes his head then thinks to himself, "I think that was the same cellmate Kaseem had!" "So, you gon hop in the shower?" Nate asked grabbing the Straight Stuntin Magazine. Justice laughed and replied, "Yea. I know wut time it is!" Justice grabs his stuff and leaves the cell. He heads to Monty's room and asks him to *watch his back in the shower. "I got you homie!" Monty drops everything and heads out behind Justice. Monty's a nineteen year old kid. Skinny with long braids. He got locked up and sentenced to four consecutive life bids for killing a judge, for his father. Nate. "Aye cuz!" Monty says to Justice as he steps into the shower. "What's up?" "You know O.G. got a nice set up for you to get Dante!" Monty replies rubbing his hands together. Justice washes his face. "Yea cuz, what they did to my brother was very disrespectful!" Monty put his left hand on his forehead. "Yea man, they were ruthless. We definitely gon help you get your revenge cuz. We gon make it to where there is no gang beef tho, so we all don't get split up and sent to different jails!" Justice looks at the door as he continues washing. "Yea man. I hear you. No trail!" Justice finishes washing up then grabs his towel* and heads out the bathroom with Monty. "You a cool young kid man. Why you stuck in dis place?" Justice asks while putting on his clothes in the locker room. "Helping my pops man. After my grandparents got killed by MS 13's, my dad and his brother went out to seek revenge!" Monty replied, starting to get angry. "Damn man, sorry to hear about your grandparents!" Justice said getting ready to leave the locker room. "No problem, cuz!" Monty turned and they started walking back to the room. "So, you really kidnapped homegirl and robbed that cash?" Monty asked looking at Justice like he was gangsta. "Yea man, but it was Kaseem's idea. I ain't want to do it but, I got his back, you know!" Monty looks forward and smiles. "Yea, loyalty to family, always a must!" They both get back to Justice's room, where Nate starts to fill them in on how to get Dante......

KASEEM

......"How are you feeling today, honey?"
Nurse Cynthia asked Kaseem as she walked
in to change his bed sheets. Kaseem didn't
respond. He just sat there in his wheelchair,
staring out the window, depressed. "Do you
need anything?" Kaseem stayed silent as he
tried to shift positions in his seat. "Here...Let
me help you!" "NO!" Kaseem lashed out,
traumatized. Nurse Cynthia jumped back.
She reassured him that everything was ok.
"No...Nothing's ever gonna be ok. You ever
had your buns took?" Kaseem yelled. You
can see hurt, pain and pure violation
written all over him. Cynthia walks over to
him and slowly rubs his back. "Trust me. I've
been doing this for eight years. It is very
disturbing what inmates have to go through

but, look on the bright side, you're alive and you're healing very fast!" Kaseem looks outside the window and sheds a tear, "It's humiliating!" He puts his head down. Cynthia goes to fluff his pillows then, give him a cup of water and two pills. "My brother Kody and my nephew Dante are truly pieces of shit. You didn't deserve what they did to you!" Kaseem quickly looked at her then, looked at his cup. "Bitch, you tryna kill me?" He yelled, throwing the water and pills onto the floor. Cynthia laughs and calmly replies, "I've been taking care of you this whole time. If I wanted to, I would've been did it already!" She chuckles then leaves the room. "I gotta let Justice know what's goin on!" He says to himself. Realizing that kidnapping the girl was Kody's niece, Kaseem didn't want what happened to him happen to his brother. Knowing that this crime was his fault from the beginning, Kaseem started thinking of *ways to get revenge on Kody, Dante, the two guys and the nurse. "Everyone has to go!" Kaseem says with an evil tone. "First, I need to fully heal!" Kaseem looks around the room for tools to make shanks out of so he doesn't get caught slipping again......*

JUSTICE

......"You got the lock?" Justice asks Monty while grabbing the three ice picks he made out of the bucket handles. "Yea, cuz and the socks!" Monty replies smiling. They sneek out of Monty's room at exactly 10:30pm. That's the time Dante and his two guys always leave to head to the laundry room. Justice heads down the hallway with Monty close by. He hands Monty the ice pick and signals him to slow down as they

come up to the corner. Justice slowly looks and sees an officer turning and disappearing around another corner. "All we gotta do is run up and hit the elevator button!" Monty says getting ready. "We'll be sitting ducks tho, jus waiting!" Justice replies, hoping not to get caught. Monty quickly sprints around the corner, presses the down button and sprints back. "Jus keep watch and when the light shines from the elevator, we out!" Monty says catching his breath. Justice daps him up then waits. "Aiight...Let's go!" They dipped to the elevator, hopped in and quickly pressed the close button. All of a sudden, they heard a voice, "Hey...Who's dat?" The door closed just in time. "Now...We gotta be very fast!" Monty says getting excited. "Yea...We gotta take the stairs coming back, too!" Justice replies. The door opens. "C'mon...This way!" Monty said as he took *a right and ran down the long hallway. He took the first left and the first double doors on the right flew open. "Yea blood, we gon get Justice, man. He jus be hiding behind that fake ass crip Monty tho!" Dante says laughing with the two guys. Monty is behind the door getting mad but, they don't even see him. "I'ma take a quick piss and I'ma be back. Don't mess up my sheets!" Dante yells walking away. Monty holds the door so, he won't be seen by him. Justice quickly slides right past Monty and through the doors. Justice hops into the dirty laundry bin as Monty hides behind it. The two guys grab and seperate the sheets. One of the guys opens the dryer doors and places wet sheets in there as the other guy walks away. Justice looks, hops out and quietly sneeks up on him. He pokes the guy in the neck, twice and lifts him up to place him in the dryer. The other guy comes back* and sees Justice closing the dryer. "What the!" The guy gets stabbed in the back by Monty. Justice gets close to the guy and whispers, "Don't worry...This is only gonna hurt alot!" Justice grabs a broomstick, breaks it and shoves it down the guys throat. "Ha ha ha! Ruthless, cuz!" Monty says extra excited as they both put him in the dryer and place lots of sheets in it. "Let's go!" Justice replies. They burst open the door, dip to the right, where Dante headed, made it to the door that had the sign stairs. "I think it's four flights up or three!" Monty said looking confused. "Let's jus go!" Justice shouted as he pushed the door open and took off up the stairs. "Yea...It's four!" Monty yells as they get three flights up. "You sure?" Justice asked yelling back, trying to catch his breath. Monty didn't reply, he just kept running. Justice made it to the door and stopped dead in his tracks. "What's wrong?" Monty asked. "Look!" Justice said quietly. About fifteen to twenty officers scrambling around trying to find out who killed two men. "Emergency lockdown. All inmates return to your rooms!" From the loud speaker. "What are we gonna do now?" Justice asked worried. "Jus wait until we see an opening!" Monty replied with his face stuck to the glass. A few minutes later, there were only three officers. They were walking together in a straight line. "When they turn their backs, we gon take a left into that small hallway!" Monty said quietly. "Let's go!" Monty quietly opened the door and they rushed to the hallway. "Damn!" Monty said pissed off. "What's wrong now?" Justice asked looking around. "We're on the wrong side of the building!" Monty replied shaking his head. "Then where are we?" As soon as Justice asked *that question, they turned into a room and seen a tall, slim, white guy with glasses, leaning back against his desk, receiving oral from a black kid. "Do you mind?" The white guy said, waving them off. "Davon!" Monty shouted. Davon takes the piece out of his mouth, licks his lips and turns his head. "What...I need color pencils!" He turns his head back and continues his payment. "Dis kid has no respect for himself!" Monty replies shaking his head. They rush out the room and sneek past an officer and end up in Dante's room. Dante's facing the wall, with headphones on, listening to the radio, when they quietly rush him. "Stop playin...What the!" Dante says confused. "Goodnight!" Justice whispers as he hits Dante over the head with the lock in a sock. They beat on him for about thirty seconds until Monty says, "Let's go!" He sees the rage in Justice's eyes and realizes he couldn't convince him. "Hey...Make sure you make it back safe!" Monty whispers as he sneeks out and disappears. Justice, with no hesitation, rips Dante's clothes off. He pulls Dante to the floor and ties his hands to the bottom of the bunk. He puts a small sock in his mouth and ties a long sock around his mouth, for complete silence. He throws water on him to wake him up. After two cold cups, Dante wakes up and shakes his face. "Hmm, hmm!" Is all Dante can get out. Justice pulls out a razor from his mouth, looks at Dante and whispers, "This is for Sasha and her twins!" He slowly slides the razor down to the base of his manhood and looks at him. Without a blink, Justice presses down and slides all the way out, staring at Dante's big, painful, hurt, waterflowing eyes. He looks down and sees blood gushing all over his hand and Dante's* body. Justice smiles as he hears Dante's muffled screams. "Have you ever seen a hotdog split open, down the middle?" He asked Dante. Dante, still in shock and screaming for his life, tries to break free. "This is for my brother!" He whispers as he grabs Dante's leg and lifts it. Dante doesn't fight back because he's too sensitive. Justice asks as he smiles and looks at Dante's face, "Any last words?" Justice, with the razor in his right hand, grabs Dante's left cheek and places the razor on his anal cavity. Dante tries to brace himself because he knows this is going to be bad. Dante takes deep breaths and Justice just presses down and slides his hand all the way to the middle part of Dante's back. Justice drops Dante's leg, throws the razor in the toilet and flushes it. As soon as he's finished washing his hands, he walks out and forgets about the three officers in the hallway......

O.G. MASTER KODY

......Kody is standing over Dante, with anger and disappointment. "You got caught slippin for real nephew!" Dante is laying in the hospital bed with tubes all in him. Cynthia comes walking in with extra sheets and a bed pan, to empty Dante's bladder. "Thanks, sis!" Kody says sadly rubbing her shoulder. "Don't thank me. I'm jus doin my job!" She replies with a stank attitude. "What was that?" Kody asked, giving her a sharp, evil look. "Did it ever occur to you that all the stuff you guys do, it will eventually come back?" Cynthia replied as she snapped her neck and began to untwist the tube to drain the urine. "You're right and that's what's gonna happen to Kaseem and Justice!" Kody looked out the window, thinking when it's going to be the right time to get at nthem. "And what did they do sooo wrong to get on all of you guys bad side?" She asked with her hand on her hip, waiting for a lame excuse. "They're the one's who kidnapped your daughter!" Cynthia dropped the pan and piss flew everywhere. "Oh my god!" Kody laughed and said, "You honestly didn't know?" Cynthia starts shaking. "Her father and brother knows, right?" Kody continues to stare out the window. "Yea...They know. I don't talk to them much, tho!" Cynthia cleans up the mess and changes the bag. "You guys need to stop this. Ya'll are family!" Cynthia sits Dante's bed up so, she can put fluffier pillows under him. "Oh, it's gonna end real soon!" Kody replies in an evil tone......

ONE YEAR LATER

JUSTICE AND DENISE

......*Justice is already sitting in the chair when Denise and his son Lyfe comes to the window. This time, Justice is wearing an orange jumper and handcuffs. Denise and Lyfe are thrilled to see him but, surprised at the way he looks, "Hey, babe!" Denise says, worried that Justice hasn't been eating regularly. His face looks sunken in and his hair is long and in a messed up ponytail. Lyfe is pointing at Justice and rubbing his sheeks. "Baby, what happened?" Denise asked, concerned. "I can't say much ndbut, we're all set now!" He replies smiling. "Then, why do you look the way you do?" Denise asked sadly. "Because I'm doin two* years in seg for slicing up a kid!" Justice leans back. Lyfe kept trying to grab the phone but, Denise was trying to understand what was going on. "So, you're still getting out of here in sixteen months, right?" "Yea!" He reassured her. "I'll be out of seg two weeks before I'm released!" "So, how come you haven't been writing me?" Denise asked, crossing her arms. "We're not allowed to write, only receive mail!" Lyfe keeps putting up three fingers. "What's lil man doing now?" He asked smiling at him. "You ask him!" Denise hands the phone to Lyfe. "Daddy!" He yells. "What up big man? How you been?" Lyfe covers the phone and replies, "I jus turned three again. Mommy said I'm four but, I said no, I'm three again!" Justice laughed. "Daddy, why you look skinny and why you have a beard and a mustache?" Justice sat up and began to explain. "Cuz daddy's in time out and when you're in time out, you're not allowed to have certain things!" Lyfe rubs his face. "But, when mommy puts me in time out, I don't have a beard and a mustache!" Both Justice and Denise laugh. The officer looked at Justice and nodded. Justice noticed and looked back at his family. "Son, listen to me, ok. I'ma be on time out fore one more birthday, ok. When I come home, I'ma make it all up to you, ok?" "You promise?" Lyfe asked with his sad little fingers rubbing the glass and his puppy light brown eyes. Justice tried to hold back tears. "I promise, Lyfe. Now keep being good and I'ma see you real soon, ok? Put mommy back on the phone!" "It's ok baby, we got this. Sasha's doin much better. She can walk now but, she still needs her bag until she can regain full muscle strength down there!" Denise holds up two fingers and Justice shakes his head. "I talk to Kaseem, once in a while, how's he really doing?" She asked. Justice shakes his head and replies, "Bad. Sometimes I think he wants to end himself cus of what happened, you know. I feel there's something he's not telling me, tho!" Justice rubs his face as he is lost for words. "You guys just need to hurry up and get out!" Justice puts a smile back on his face and nods his head. "Oh, we is definitely comin home, tho!" "Time's up!" The officer yells. Justice says his I love you's to Denise and Lyfe then hangs up as he quickly gets escorted out of the visit and back to his room......

KASEEM AND SASHA

......Tears rushed down Kaseem's face when he seen Sasha walk up to the window with a cane. She still had her glow and she was excited to see Kaseem. Sasha just didn't have the belly anymore and she couldn't sit down. Kaseem stood up and grabbed the phone. "Say something, baby!" Sasha said as tears ran down her face. Kaseem just looked at her and was ashamed of himself to let this happen to her. Every emotion he had, he couldn't let out because he didn't want the officers to see. "I'm sorry for everything, baby!" He replied in a low tone, rubbing on the window. She rubbed back. "If I never did this B & E, none of this would've happened to you!" Sasha looked confused. "What do you mean?" Kaseem looked in her beautiful light brown eyes and replied, "The young girl that we kidnapped, her whole family is in here. They know all about us!" Kaseem put his head down, ashamed. "Are you and Justice ok?" She asked looking at his neck to see if he had any marks or bruises. "Yea, I'm cool. Justice got ambushed by one of these *fake ass officers last year, tho!" He looked at them, mean mugging. "Baby...Listen!" Sasha said in a low tone. They both paused for a moment. "The doctor said I can't have any kids because of the damage from the broom!" More tears rushed down Kaseem's face. "Baby!" Sasha whispered. Kaseem didn't respond because he started getting furious. Losing his train of thought from what Kody did to him and his girl. He didn't realize she was still talking. "Baby...Do you still love me?" Sasha asked dropping a couple of tears. He looked into her watery eyes, waited a moment and replied, "I'll always love you. No matter what. I promise you, they're gonna pay for everything!" Sasha wiped her face, fixed her shirt and began to tell Kaseem about starting over when he gets out. "Baby...I have fifteen months left. We can do whatever you want!" Kaseem replies smiling. "I love you, baby. I'm not going anywhere!" She says, blowing a* kiss through the glass. "I love you too, baby. I got you!" He replies as he drops another tear and hangs up. He watches her walk away and starts thinking of a plan to end Kody's life!......

TEN MONTHS LATER

KASEEM AND KODY

......"See...The difference between me and you is...I'm willing to do it. You...You get forced!" Davon said while eating cheetos. "I'll never be like you, RIPPER!" Kaseem replied throwing a haymaker. Davon went to sleep, instantly. "I'm sick of this shit!" He said grabbing his knife and heading out the room. He heads down the hallway, passing a few rooms, when he sees Dante pulling up in his wheelchair. "You wanna ride?" Kaseem asks as he grabs the back of his chair and heads towards the stairs. "Fuck you!" Dante yells. Kaseem opens the door and kicks the chair. Dante screams as the chair flies up and he falls forward. Kaseem didn't even watch. He headed straight to Kody's room. A minute later, he gets there and Kody's laying on the bunk with a blanket over him. "Wake up, homothug!" Kaseem yells as he stabs up the body. "What the!" He realizes the blanket covered a bunch of pillows. He quickly gets rushed from behind by Kody. "Ahhh...Yea, jus how I like it!" Kody whispers in his ear. Kaseem tries to fight to get out of his hold. "Squirm, gurl. That's what I like!" Kody licks the back of Kaseem's neck. Kaseem swings his left arm and stabs Kody in his left leg. Kody tries to tighten his hands, even though the *knife went deep. Kaseem swings again and throws his head back, trying to hit Kody in the nose. He catches his leg again and Kody finally loosens up. Kaseem breaks free. "Yea...You goin down, jus like your nephew!" Kody holds his leg as blood starts to run down. Kaseem swings the knife at Kody's face. Kody quickly grabs his arm and headbutts Kaseem. Instantly, blood rushes from both nostrils. "Fuck!" Kaseem yells. He holds his nose as Kody grabs him and picks him up. Kody slams him on the floor, banging his head on the edge of the bunk. "Ha ha ha!" Kody shouts as he grabs a rag and tightens it around his leg. Kaseem, dazed from the bunk, slowly gets up, holding his head. "Uh uh!" Kody says grabbing Kaseem's left leg. He leans it up to the tiolet and has his foot rest on the seat. Kaseem, trying to come back to life as a striking blow hits him in his left cheek.*

Kody stares at Kaseem for a few seconds. "Kaseem...Kaseem!" Kody says looking at the blood running from his nose and mouth. Kaseem makes a noise, "Dat's all I need to hear!" Kody replied smiling as he leans back and donkey kicks Kaseem's leg. Breaking it to the point where the bone pokes out next to the knee cap. Kaseem screams for his life. "Shhh...That was for Dante!" Kody whispered as he pulls off kaseem's pants. "Now...If you bite me, you won't have a piece anymore!" Kody says holding a razor to Kaseem's sac. He whips out his piece and brings it to Kaseem's lips. Kaseem, still leaking and in pain, realizes he still has the knife. He looks up at Kody and quickly slices his manhood clean off. "AHHH!" Kody yells histerically, dropping the razor and backing away to the wall. Kaseem grabs onto the bunk and tries to get up. Kody drops to the floor as he sees *his piece laying there with blood running from it. An inmate runs into the room. "Damn!" He says observing everything. He looks at Kody and kicks him dead in his forehead, knocking him out. "He's been raping me too!" The inmate said to Kaseem. Kaseem looked and tried to stand. "Go get help!" He said, looking for something to wipe his face with. The inmate ran out the room and a few minutes later, he came back with officers and nurses. Kaseem looked at the inmate then past out onto the bunk!......*

......There were officers in both hospital rooms as Kaseem and Kody were getting treated. Dante rolled himself into O.G. Master Kody's room, angry as ever. "We need to do something about these brothers, man...I'm sick of this!" Kody looked at Dante then at the officers. "Listen...They're definitely going to get theirs!" Dante shook

his head and replied, "But, they go home in a few months. Kaseem's going to seg as soon as he wakes up and Justice is protected!" Kody, with his face swollen, smiled at Dante and said, "Go get your aunt, right now!" Dante leaves to grab Cynthia. He comes back with her a couple minutes later. "The answer is no for whatever your plan it!" She said with an attitude. Kody looked at Dante then, looked back at Cynthia. "Listen...The only reason this happened to me was because I heard Kaseem say he was going to kidnap your daughter again when he gets out but, this time, kill her. So, I did what I had to and he got the best of me!" Cynthia looks at Dante, upset. She gives both of them their pills, puts her head down and replies, "I really hate all of this gang stuff. That's why I don't have my daughter around you guys. My son is in here and so is his father. This needs to stop. I don't need my daughter getting caught up in anymore of this!" She starts to cry. "I will talk to my son, after this, no more!" She demanded. Cynthia stormed out of the room while Dante and Kody smiled. "Now, look...We need to pay these officers to look the other way!" Dante said rubbing his hands together. Kody replies, "I'll talk to the captain and make sure things go our way...We'll be aiight!"......

RELEASE DATE

......"TAP TAP TAP!" The officer hits Kaseem's seg door with his keys. "It's time to go!" Kaseem opens his eyes and looks at his left leg. "Damn!" He says upset. "Still in a cast!" Kaseem sits up and grabs his wheelchair. He leans on it to help himself up so, he can take *a piss and wash up. He already has everything packed and ready to go. "Yea, boi!" He shouts happily. The officer comes back five minutes later and opens the door. "You ready?" He asks, holding Kaseem's discharge papers. Kaseem sits in his chair and rolls past him. "Hell yea!" The officer walks side by side with him down the hall to the front. "You and your brother made a huge impact on this jail!" Kaseem looked at the officer and smiled. The officer leaned in and whispered in his ear, "So, when you gon tell your gurl that you became Kody's bitch?" The officer slapped him in the back of his head and dropped his papers on his lap. Kaseem quickly got upset. "Sign here!" The lady at the desk said to Kaseem as she handed him a pen and paper. He quickly signed, gave her the paper back and wheeled it out the front door. "Baby!" Sasha yelled as she waived from the back seat. Denise and Lyfe were in the front jumping* up and down. Sasha hops out and lifts the trunk. "It's about damn time!" She says as she give Kaseem a big wet kiss. She helps him into the back, closes the door and puts the wheelchair into the trunk. She gets back into the car when Kaseem asks, "Where's Justice?" They all looked back at him and replied, "He wasn't with you?" Kaseem simply asks, "What time is it?" Denise looked at her watch, "6:38am!" Kaseem leaned back, rubbed Lyfe on the head and replied, "Oh yea! Time to relax cus, he ain't getting out until 8am!" They all looked at each other, sat back and relaxed!......

......"You ok, cuz?" Monty asked Justice as he was pacing back and forth. "What time is it?" He asked, concerned. "Homie...It's one minute past the last time you asked...Jus chill!" Monty replied, flipping cards on his bed, playing solitare. "7:55am. I know they out there waiting...You sure the officer coming at 8?" Justice was starting to get on Monty's nerves. "If you don't sit yo halfway free ass down and eat a honey bun!" Monty shouted. Justice looked at him and agreed. "So, what you gon do when you get out tho?" Monty asked leaning back, pushing the cards away. "I'm gonna take a nice dump, smoke a newport one hunnit and shower this place off me!" Monty smiled and shook his head. "I can dig it, cuz!" "TAP TAP TAP!" The officer knocked on the door. "Cosgrove...Time to go!" Justice hopped up, grabbed his bag and gave Monty a hug. "Keep ya head up, man!" Monty pushed back and replied, "Make sure you write me and don't forget to send me those wedding pictures!" Justice hit the corner with the officer, laughed and replied, "Don't even trip, cuz!" Justice, with a huge smile on his face, looks at the officer and says, "So, what you gon do in about an hour...Check nuts and butts?" The officer smirks as they *approach the front desk. Justice looks outside and sees the black 2018 Cadillac. Denise, Sasha, Lyfe and Kaseem are waiving at him. "Sign here!" The lady at the desk says, handing him a pen and paper. Justice continues to look at his family and realizes they're yelling. He smiles back and waves then looks at the paper. He signs it, hands it back then turns to walk towards the door. He notices that they're pointing. Right before the sun-rays hit his face, Justice feels a sharp pain in his back. He instantly drops his bag and begins to turn around. A hand with and ice pick comes from nowhere and attacks his neck. Justice get poked twice and falls to the floor. He looks at the officer and the officer turns away, like nothing happened. Justice grabs his neck, while blood gushes out. He turns to look and sees Monty wiping the pick on his shirt. Monty steps over Justice and leans in. "Thought you were free, huh? Well...I have another surprise for you!" Justice, confused and trying to talk, starts coughing up blood and chokes. Monty bends down and starts to whisper in his ear, "The girl you kidnapped...Was my sister!" Justice rolls to his side, to see his family one last time. Monty swings his arm back and forth, poking Justice in his side and in his back until Justice stops moving. Monty feels Justice's body stiffing up. He gets up, looks at the Cadillac and waves!......*

THE END

Made in the USA
Middletown, DE
14 May 2021

38858634R00047